P9-DDD-940

I, TRIXIE who is dog

I must not chase skunks
I must not chase skunks
I must not

Dean Koontz

ILLUSTRATED BY Janet Cleland

G. P. Putnam's Sons • Penguin Young Readers Group

G. P. PUTNAM'S SONS

A division of Penguin Young Readers Group.

Published by The Penguin Group. Penguin Group (USA) Inc., 375 Hudson Street, New York, NY 10014, U.S.A. Penguin Group (Canada), 90 Eglinton Avenue East, Suite 700, Toronto, Ontario M4P 2Y3, Canada (a division of Pearson Penguin Canada Inc.). Penguin Books Ltd, 80 Strand, London WC2R 0RL, England. Penguin Ireland, 25 St. Stephen's Green, Dublin 2, Ireland (a division of Penguin Books Ltd.). Penguin Group (Australia), 250 Camberwell Road, Camberwell, Victoria 3124, Australia (a division of Pearson Australia Group Pty Ltd). Penguin Books India Pvt Ltd, 11 Community Centre, Panchsheel Park, New Delhi - 110 017, India. Penguin Group (NZ), 67 Apollo Drive, Rosedale, North Shore 0632, New Zealand (a division of Pearson New Zealand Ltd). Penguin Books (South Africa) (Pty) Ltd, 24 Sturdee Avenue, Rosebank, Johannesburg 2196, South Africa. Penguin Books Ltd, Registered Offices: 80 Strand, London WC2R 0RL, England.

Design by Richard Amari.

Text set in Gothic Blond Husky.

The art was done in watercolor and pen and ink.

Library of Congress Cataloging-in-Publication Data

Koontz, Dean R. (Dean Ray), 1945– I, Trixie who is dog / Dean Koontz ; illustrated by Janet Cleland. p. cm. Summary: The author's golden retriever explains why she is delighted to be a dog. [1. Dogs—Fiction.] I. Cleland, Janet, ill. II. Title. PZ7.K83574Iam 2009 [E]—dc22 2008053358

ISBN 978-0-399-25196-2

1 3 5 7 9 10 8 6 4 2

Bliss to you. Bliss to you!
Is me, who is dog,
Trixie Koontz, happy dog.

Dog is the best of the best things to be.
Sorry you are not dog.
Not everyone can be.

Not everyone should be
or could be
or would be a dog.

Some must be people,
 to feed all good dogs.
People to pet dogs,
 people to scratch,
to chase and play catch.

MEYOWRRR

Some must be cats,
　　'cause cats make dogs laugh.
Caterwauling,
　　catapulting,
　　　catnapping cats.

—WOO-HOO!

Some must be birds,
to make dogs dream of flying.
Blackbirds and bluebirds,
striped birds and who birds.

Some must be cows,
so dogs can have ice cream.

White cows and gray cows,
    night cows and day cows,
        happy cows dancing the waltz and the tango.

Some must be sheep,
so dogs can herd them,
and shave them
to make warm woolen sweaters
for wild wintry nights.

Some must be skunks,
　　but I don't know why.
　　　They stink, *really* stink—
　　　　and they can't play the banjo.

I, Trixie Koontz, was dog, am dog,
always will be dog,
swimming and running
and playing the banjo.
Playing the banjo is bliss.

Bliss, food is bliss!
Food is as good
as a good thing can be.
Kibble! Cookies!
Carrots! Chicken!

One day I will learn to cook and to bake.
Muffins and cakes.
French fries and pies.

Then at the table I'll take a seat.
And eat.
And eat.
And eat.

After eating or even before,
I like a belly rub—
then one more.
Cows seldom get belly rubs.
Skunks never do.
Because—oh, *pew*!

My next-door neighbor,
    wiener dog Jinx,
        has a long tummy,
           a rub-a-dub tummy.
Lucky dog,
    wiener dog,
        long-tummy Jinx.

LEMONADE 50¢

SPLAT!

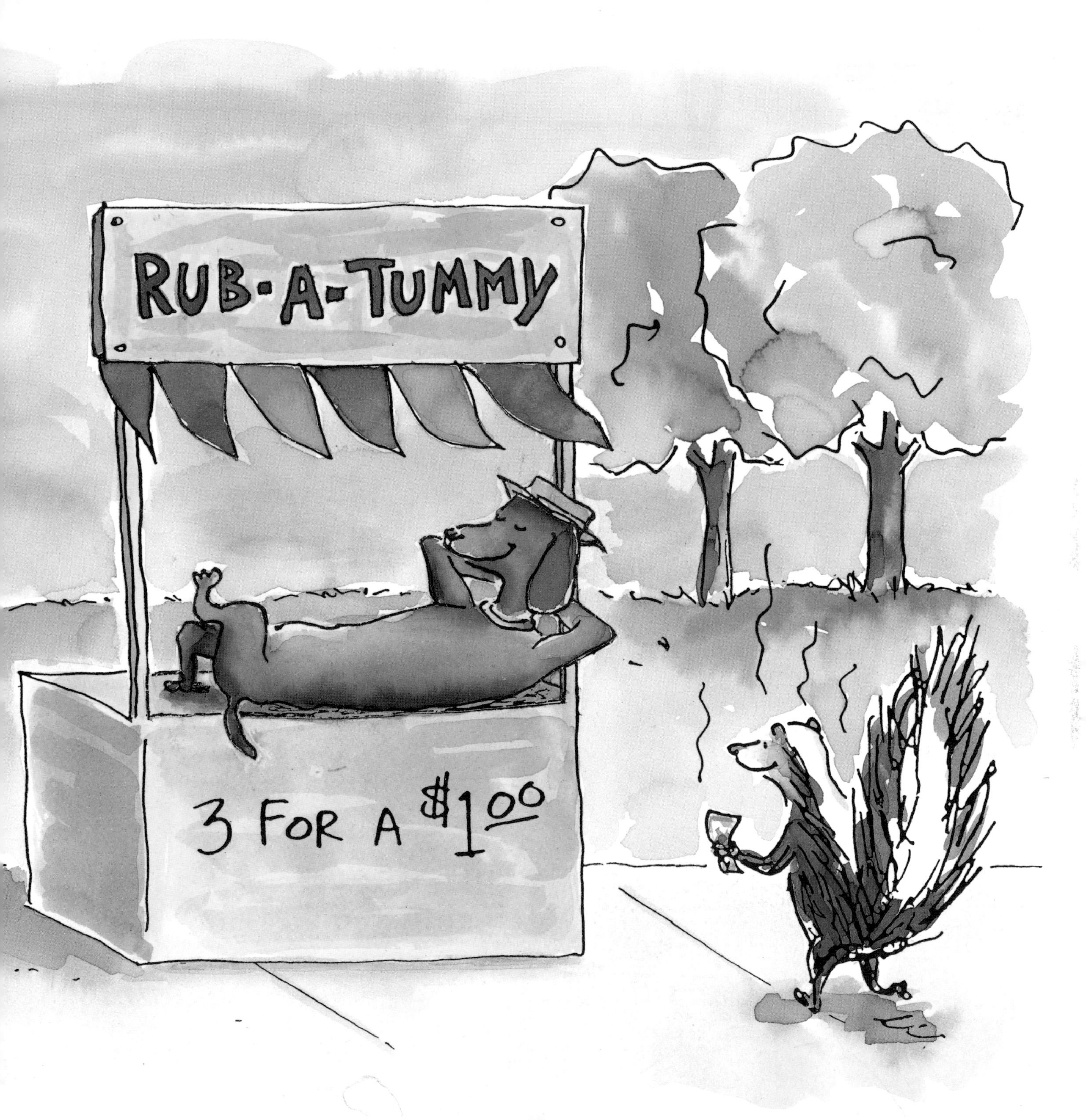
RUB-A-TUMMY
3 FOR A $1.00

I, Trixie, have a dream,
a fine dream,
as every dog does.

Want to drive a car on the open road.
Me and Jinx on a long desert road
where coyotes sell milk shakes
in cactus cafés.

Drive far up north,
  where strange snowmen roam,
    where mooses are nice to
      dogs far from home.

And way down south,
  eating chicken and grits,
    with fat friendly gators
      in Panama hats.

But law doesn't allow dogs
to drive cars.
I wonder if law
is more fair on Mars.

Maybe in emergency,
        might be okay to drive.
Like when Jinx eats all the peanut butter in the jar,
        and gets his snout stuck,
            it's in there so far.
                Or he sits on his master's false teeth.

Then we're off to the vet
 at high speed in the car,
  with the teeth in his butt
   and his snout in the jar.

We good dogs are loyal and brave and true.
We do everything,
mostly,
we're told to do.

So I won't drive a car.
But you know what I think?
Not even a skunk would make a stink . . .
if I drove a *bus*!

Dog is the best of the best things to be.
Maybe you're not dog.
Maybe you are.
Whatever you are is the best thing to be
if you have a dream and your dream is big.

Bliss to Jinx.
Bliss to you.
Bliss to me.